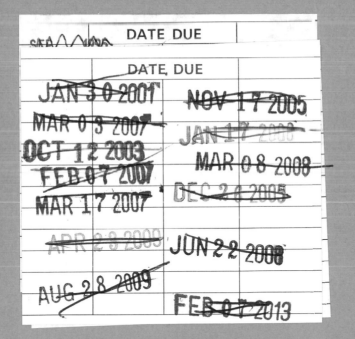

How Rabbit Tricked Otter

AND OTHER CHEROKEE TRICKSTER STORIES

Told by GAYLE ROSS • Illustrated by MURV JACOB

With a Foreword by CHIEF WILMA MANKILLER

HarperCollins*Publishers*

Cop. 1

This collection is lovingly dedicated to my nieces and nephews,
Lauren, John, James, Mary, and Michelle.
And most especially, for my own children, Alan and Sarah.

—GR

To my wife, Debbie, and my mother, Maxine,
For all your love and support.

—MJ

This title is derived from a series of Native American tales documenting representative tribal cultures in the United States and Canada. The Parabola Storytime Series ® has been developed and produced by *Parabola Magazine* in collaboration with leading Native American artists, storytellers, and musicians. Audio versions are available from HarperAudio.

• •

How Rabbit Tricked Otter
And Other Cherokee Trickster Stories
Text copyright © 1994 by Gayle Ross
Illustrations copyright © 1994 by Murv Jacob

Library of Congress Cataloging-in-Publication Data
Ross, Gayle.
How Rabbit tricked Otter and other Cherokee trickster stories / told by Gayle Ross ; illustrated by Murv Jacob ; with a foreword by Chief Wilma Mankiller.
p.   cm.
Summary: Fifteen traditional tales follow the adventures of Rabbit, the Cherokee trickster.
ISBN 0-06-021285-3. — ISBN 0-06-021286-1 (lib. bdg.)
1. Cherokee Indians—Legends. 2. Rabbit (Legendary character)—Legends.   [1. Rabbit (Legendary character)
2. Cherokee Indians—Legends. 3. Indians of North America—Legends.]   I. Jacob, Murv, ill.   II. Title.
E99.C5R66 1994   93-3637
398.2'089'975—dc20   CIP
                                                                                                                              AC

Typography by Tom Starace
1 2 3 4 5 6 7 8 9 10
❖
First Edition

CONTENTS

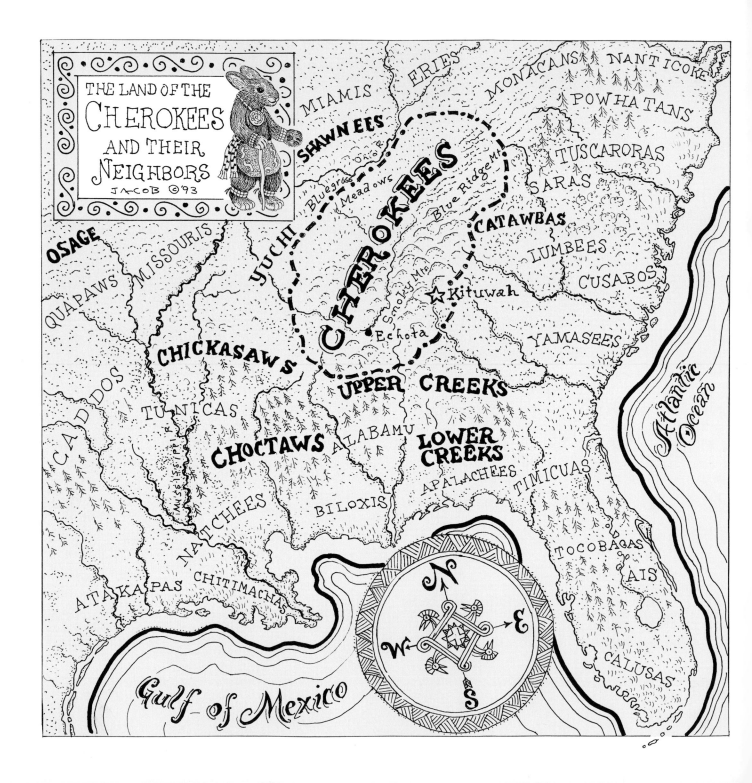

FOREWORD

When I was a child growing up in the isolated Cherokee community of Mankiller Flats, we had no telephone, television, or other direct link to the outside world except a battery-operated radio. Like generations of Cherokees before us, we relied on storytelling to pass cultural and historical information from generation to generation. Storytelling was also a great way for adults to entertain others, especially young people, and to teach important value lessons about honesty, personal responsibility, and the importance of sharing with others.

From tiny Alaskan Native villages to the Great Iroquois Nation, Native people have an astounding array of wonderful stories. As long as these stories survive, the oral histories of Native people will survive.

No stories are more important in the Cherokee oral tradition than the stories of Rabbit, the trickster-hero. Gayle Ross and Murv Jacob have contributed greatly to the preservation of the stories of Rabbit by creating this wonderful collection of stories and illustrations. These stories will help the reader appreciate the art of storytelling in this highly technological age.

—Chief Wilma Mankiller,
Principal Chief of the Cherokee Nation

Flint Visits Rabbit

This is what the old people told me when I was a child, about the days when the people and the animals still spoke the same language. Now in those days, the animals had a society that was organized very much like the people's. They had great chiefs. They held councils and stickball games. Each animal had his place. Buzzard was known as a great doctor, while Turtle knew the secrets of conjuring. Frog was the marshall at the council house. Rabbit's job was to be the messenger. He was to spread important news. He was also a good singer and often led in the dance. But Rabbit was the leader of them all in mischief, and his bold ways were

. . . .

always getting him into trouble.

At that time, there lived a great stone giant named Old Flint. All the people used to travel into the mountains to find Flint, and to chip pieces from his body to make their arrowheads and spearpoints. In this way Old Flint helped to kill the animals, and they hated him for it. Often the animals talked of getting rid of Old Flint, but everyone was so frightened of him that no one had ever climbed up the mountain where he lived. At last, they called a great council to talk over means of putting Flint out of the way.

Rabbit stood up in the council house and began to speak. "Why is everybody here so afraid?" he asked. "Why, it would be no more than half a day's work for a mighty warrior like myself to rid the world of Flint. If you are all so frightened, I will kill him!" Rabbit boasted. Now, Rabbit was speaking mostly because he liked the sound of his own voice. But when he saw how impressed the other animals were with his bravery, he began to believe his own words. The very next day, Rabbit set out to climb the mountain where Old Flint lived.

· ·

Rabbit climbed and climbed, and he was almost to Flint's house when he realized he did not know what he would do when he got there. "I should have a plan," said Rabbit. He sat down to think, but no ideas came to him. At last, Rabbit decided that he would greet Flint and then, according to Cherokee custom, Flint would have to invite Rabbit into his house and offer him something to eat. "Once I am inside his house," thought Rabbit, "then I'll have an idea." He continued up the mountain.

Flint was standing in his doorway when Rabbit came up and said, "*Osiyo*—hello. Are you the one they call Flint?"

Flint said, "Yes, that is my name."

"Well, is this where you live?" asked Rabbit.

"Yes," said Flint, "this is my house." Rabbit stood there, looking about and waiting for Flint to invite him inside and offer him some food. After all, custom was very strict about this. But apparently Flint's manners were bad. He just stood there, looking down at Rabbit.

After a time, Rabbit said, "My name is Rabbit; I expect you have heard of me." Flint said that he had not heard of Rabbit. "Well, it's because I am so well known as a good cook that I thought you might have heard of me. I have just come to invite you to visit." Rabbit had decided that if Flint would come to his house, Rabbit could find a way to catch him off guard.

When Flint explained that he never left his mountain, Rabbit began to talk about the food he could prepare. "Well, maybe I will visit you someday," said Flint.

"Why not come tomorrow?" said Rabbit. "You could have supper with me." Rabbit coaxed and coaxed, and at last Flint agreed. "Good," said Rabbit. "I live in the broom-grass field, right next to the river." Rabbit scurried back down the mountain, and he worked hard all night long, gathering and preparing many different kinds of food.

The next day, Rabbit had such a great feast laid out in front of his hole that when Flint came down from his mountain, he asked, "How many people are coming for dinner?"

Rabbit said, "Well, I didn't know what you liked to eat best, so I

· ·

fixed a lot of different kinds of food."

Flint and Rabbit sat down to eat, and it wasn't long before Rabbit was full. But Flint had never seen so many different kinds of food before. Every time he thought he was full, he saw something he hadn't tried yet, and he just had to have a taste of it. While Flint was busy eating, Rabbit got two sticks of wood and began to carve them into a sharp wooden wedge and a great wooden mallet.

"What are those for?" asked Flint suspiciously.

"Oh, you know me," said Rabbit. "I'm just the kind of fellow who likes to keep busy, and you never know when tools will come in handy!"

At last Flint had eaten so much that he could scarcely move, and his belly was greatly swollen. He said to Rabbit, "Maybe I should rest a while before I climb back up that mountain."

"Stay," said Rabbit. "Visit as long as you like." It wasn't long before Flint had stretched out in the broom-grass field and fallen sound asleep.

Rabbit spoke to Flint a few times to make sure he was asleep.

HOW RABBIT TRICKED OTTER

. . . .

Then he crept over and put that wooden wedge on Flint's great belly. With one sharp blow of the mallet, Rabbit drove the wedge into Flint. Then he turned and ran for his hole as fast as he could go.

Suddenly, the ground began to shake with a terrible explosion. Rabbit dove into his hole and listened as the pieces of Flint's body rained down all over the earth. When everything was quiet, he put out his head to look; and one last sharp sliver of Flint fell and *phht,* split Rabbit's nose right down the middle.

And that is why the people no longer have to travel all the way to that mountain to make their arrowheads and spearpoints. You can find pieces of Flint lying around most everywhere.

And to this day, when you look at Rabbit's grandchildren, you will see they all have split noses still.

How Rabbit Tricked Otter

L ong ago, the animals did many of the same things that people do. They especially loved to dance. One time, the animals decided to hold a dance to honor the animal with the most beautiful fur coat. They called a great council, and they talked for a long time about whom to honor at the honor dance. Some animals had short fur, while others were covered with long, silky hair. Some animals had spots; some had stripes. Raccoon boasted of the stripes on his tail, and Skunk was especially proud of his brilliant black-and-white fur. But finally, it was decided that the animal with the most beautiful fur coat was Otter.

Now, Rabbit was the messenger. This meant it was his job to

· · · · · · · · · · · · ·

travel up the river, tell Otter about the dance, and bring him back down to the council house. Rabbit knew that his own fur coat was nothing very special, although he was quite proud of the long curly tail Creator had given him. Nevertheless, it made him jealous that Otter was going to have an honor dance. As Rabbit traveled up the river to Otter's house, more and more he thought what a funny joke it would be if he could trick Otter into staying away from the dance and fool everyone into thinking that *he* was Otter. There was only one way to do that, and that was to steal Otter's fur coat.

Rabbit reached Otter's house and told him about the dance. Otter is a very shy and humble fellow, and it made his heart feel good to know that the animals wanted to honor him in this way. He agreed to travel back down the river with Rabbit to the council house.

They hadn't gone very far when Rabbit decided to camp for the night. "This is a sacred place," Rabbit said. "It will be good for you to sleep and dream in such a place the night before you dance. Something happens here that doesn't happen anywhere else in the world. Sometimes, at night, fire falls out of the sky. That's what they call this place—the 'Fire Falling from the Sky Spot.'"

Otter had never heard of the "Fire Falling from the Sky Spot," but then he had not traveled very much. He thought maybe Rabbit knew more about these kinds of things. And so he listened when Rabbit told him what to do.

"Take off your fur coat," said Rabbit, "and hang it in a tree away from the river. You wouldn't want the falling fire to burn a hole in it. And when you go to sleep, lie down right next to the water. If the fire falls from the sky, jump in the river, and you will be safe."

Otter took off his fur coat and hung it in a tree. And when he went to sleep, he stretched out right beside the river. Rabbit waited, and when Otter was sound asleep, Rabbit took a curved piece of bark and scraped all the coals from the campfire into it. Then, standing over Otter, he threw the coals into the air as high as he could.

"Fire, falling from the sky!" cried Rabbit. Otter saw the coals raining down, and he jumped into the river. Rabbit snatched Otter's fur coat and ran.

The next day, Rabbit was back at the council house, and there was no sign of Otter. When the sun went down, the fire in the council house was built into a great roaring blaze. The drums began to play, and the singers called for everyone to dance.

Meanwhile, Rabbit disguised himself as Otter. First, he pulled down his long ears and tied them into a knot underneath his chin. Then he eased into Otter's coat. Rabbit thought he looked pretty good. He was just coming out to lead the honor dance into the council house when he remembered something. He stopped and thought about his nose, with that split running right down the middle. If the animals saw Rabbit's nose, they would know he wasn't Otter.

So Rabbit put one paw over his nose, and that's how he danced all night long. When anyone asked him what he was doing, Rabbit just said, "This is the latest dance." And since everyone had gathered to honor Otter, they respected his strange dance, and pretty soon all the animals were dancing with one paw over their noses.

Except for Bear. Bear was a good friend of Otter's, and all evening the idea grew in Bear's mind that this was not his friend. So when Bear saw his chance, he danced over to Rabbit and knocked that paw away. Everyone saw Rabbit's split nose, and with one voice, they screamed, "Rabbit!" Rabbit threw Otter's coat down and ran. But Bear was so angry that Rabbit would play such a mean trick on Otter that when Rabbit dashed by, Bear reached out with his great paw and snatched Rabbit's long, curly tail right off.

The other animals took Otter's coat and began traveling up the river to look for him. They found Otter coming toward the council house, and he was glad to get his coat back. But he wasn't very sorry about missing his dance. Something new had come into Otter's life. Until Rabbit had tricked him into jumping into the river, Otter had never been swimming, and he discovered that he liked it better than anything else.

So if you are looking for Otter's grandchildren, look in the rivers and the lakes and the streams. Because all the otters are living there still.

And even now, you will see that Rabbit's grandchildren do not have the beautiful tail that Creator gave them. All that is left is a little white puff of fur.

Why Possum's Tail Is Bare

L ong ago in the beginning days of the world, Possum didn't look the way he does now. Creator gave Possum a beautiful, bushy, furry tail, and Possum was vain about this tail. He bragged about it all the time and sang about it at every dance, until Rabbit (who didn't have much of a tail left since Bear had pulled his off) became jealous and decided to play a trick on Possum.

Rabbit went to the other animals and said, "Let's have an honor dance for Possum's tail." But all the other animals said, "We are tired of hearing Possum sing about his tail."

"If we have an honor dance for Possum," said Rabbit, "and we let him sing about his tail all night, perhaps he will not talk about it so much from now on." Well, the other animals said they had never thought about it quite like that, and maybe Rabbit was right. And so they agreed to have an honor dance for Possum's tail.

Rabbit traveled to Possum's house and gave him the news. "You mean I can sit where everyone can see me?" said Possum.

"Oh, yes," said Rabbit. "You will have a special seat of honor right next to the council fire."

"Do you mean I can sing and dance and talk about my tail all night?" asked Possum.

"Oh, yes," said Rabbit. "That's what the dance is for, to honor your beautiful tail!"

Well, of course this pleased Possum very much, and he said that he would come. Rabbit said, "I will send Cricket to you on the day of the dance, to comb and brush the fur on your tail so it will look its best." Possum liked this idea as well.

WHY POSSUM'S TAIL IS BARE

· ·

So Rabbit went to Cricket, who is such an expert haircutter that the Cherokee word for him means "the barber." Rabbit told him exactly how to fix the hair on Possum's tail.

On the day of the dance, Cricket went to Possum's house. Possum stretched out and closed his eyes and Cricket began to comb and brush the fur on Possum's tail, until it was its silkiest and shiniest. "Possum," said Cricket, "I'm going to wind a red string around the fur on your tail, very very tight, all the way to the tip. It will keep the hair smooth until it is time for you to dance. Remember, Possum, don't take the string off until just before you dance!"

That night, when the sun went down, the drums began to play and the singers to call. Everyone gathered at the council house. Possum sat in a special seat of honor, right next to the council fire, where the light was brightest.

Soon the other animals began to call, "Possum, dance! Possum, dance!" So Possum reached around behind him and pulled off the red string. With that, every hair on his tail fell off, but Possum didn't know it. He leaped into the circle of firelight and began to dance, singing, "See my beautiful bushy, furry tail!" The animals began to laugh. Possum sang, "See how it sweeps the ground!" And the animals laughed louder.

Possum decided maybe they hadn't heard him right, and so he sang louder, and the animals laughed harder. Finally, Possum realized that something must be wrong. He looked around behind him, and instead of the beautiful bushy, furry tail that he had always known, there was a long, red, skinny, hairless tail. Possum was so surprised and humiliated, all he could do was fall to the ground and grin helplessly, which Possum still does whenever you take him by surprise. And Possum's grandchildren all have red, skinny, hairless tails to this very day.

Rabbit Escapes from the Wolves

A long time ago, when the people and the animals still spoke the same language, Rabbit lay sleeping in the forest. He was having a very good dream. In his dream, Rabbit was at a dance and all the people had asked him to lead the songs. He was having a fine time, showing off his voice and watching all the pretty girls dance. In his dream, the dancers were crowding closer and closer until one of them actually stepped on his foot!

RABBIT ESCAPES FROM THE WOLVES

. . . .

Rabbit's eyes flew open and he found that he was surrounded by wolves, laughing and poking him. "Wake up, Rabbit!" said a wolf. "We are going to eat you!"

Rabbit thought very quickly. "Oh, it's that way, is it?" said Rabbit. "I wasn't sleeping. My eyes were closed because I was thinking about a new dance I know. If you were not in such a hurry to eat I could teach it to you."

Well, everybody knows that wolves love to sing, but Rabbit knew they also love to dance. Sure enough, the wolves let Rabbit up and formed a circle around him while he got ready to sing. Rabbit made a great show of clearing his throat and preening his fur. At last, he began patting his feet and humming. Then he started to dance around in a circle. Finally, he began to sing:

"Tlage'situn' gali'sgi'sida'ha
Ha'nia lil! lil! Ha'nia lil! lil!
On the edge of the field I dance about—
Ha'nia lil! lil! Ha'nia lil! lil!"

The wolves began to dance in a circle around Rabbit, following

his steps. Rabbit called, "When I sing 'edge of the field,' I will dance in that direction!" Rabbit began the song again, and this time his dance steps took him toward the field. "Now," said Rabbit, "this time when I sing *lil! lil!* you must all close your eyes and stomp your feet hard!"

The wolves thought this was a fine dance, so Rabbit began another round singing the same song. When he sang "edge of the field," he danced that way; and when he sang *lil! lil!* the wolves closed their eyes and stomped their feet. Rabbit sang louder and louder. He kept on dancing closer and closer to the field. At last, on the fourth round of songs, when the wolves were stomping as hard as they could and thinking only of the dance, Rabbit made one long jump and was off through the long grass.

Rabbit scurried through the grass, twisting and turning, as fast as he could. The wolves were after him at once, however, and they are very swift runners. Rabbit was almost out of breath when he spied a hollow tree trunk. He dove through a hole at the roots and climbed up the inside of the trunk.

When the wolves reached the tree, they began arguing about the best way to get Rabbit out of that trunk. Finally, one of them put his head through the hole and peered up at Rabbit. But Rabbit spit right into his eye, and the wolf had to pull his head out. Now, spitting on someone is a way to put a powerful curse on them, and the wolves were becoming frightened! When no other wolf wanted to put his head in the hole, they all went away and left Rabbit hiding in the trunk. When he was sure it was safe, Rabbit climbed out and went on about his business.

HOW DEER WON HIS ANTLERS

I n the very beginning days of the world, Deer had no antlers. His head was as smooth as a doe's. Deer was a great runner and Rabbit was a great jumper. Everyone was always arguing over which one was the faster, and finally it was decided that the two must run a race to settle the matter once and for all.

Rabbit was always one to boast, and he was eager to prove that he was faster than Deer. But Deer was very shy, and he had no interest in racing Rabbit. Finally, someone hit on the idea of carving a beautiful pair of antlers as a prize for the winner. When Deer saw the antlers, he knew he would look splendid wearing them, and so he agreed to the race. It was decided that Rabbit and Deer would start together on one side of the thicket, race through it, and come back. Whoever came out first would be the winner.

On the day of the race, all the animals gathered at the thicket. The antlers were put down on the ground, so that everyone could admire them. While they were looking at the horns, Rabbit said, "I don't know this part of the country so well. I want to take a look through the bushes where I'm supposed to run."

Everyone thought that would be all right, so Rabbit disappeared into the thicket. But he was gone so long that at last the animals suspected that Rabbit was up to one of his tricks. They sent Mole to dig under the ground, into the thicket, to see what Rabbit was doing.

Mole dug his way underground until he had reached the middle of the thicket. When he came up, he found Rabbit gnawing down the low bushes and pulling them away, until he had a nice clear road to run on, a sort of tunnel through the thicket all the way to the other side!

Mole turned around and came back and told the other animals

what Rabbit was doing. When Rabbit finally came back, they all accused him of cheating. Rabbit pretended to be very hurt. "Why should I cheat?" said Rabbit. "Everyone knows that I will win. You are just jealous because you know that when I wear the antlers I will not only be the fastest animal, I will also be the handsomest."

"Why were you gone so long, then?" asked Deer. "And what do you say about what Mole saw?"

"Oh, I was just studying the thicket very carefully," said Rabbit. "And everyone knows that Mole can't see very well. He always has dirt in his eyes."

Rabbit kept insisting that he was not cheating, until the others took him into the thicket, and there was the cleared road, just as Mole had said. Everyone agreed that a cheater had no right to enter the race at all, and so they gave the beautiful antlers to Deer, who has worn them proudly ever since.

The other animals told Rabbit that since he was so fond of cutting down bushes, he could just as well do that for a living. And so he does, to this day.

WHY DEER'S TEETH ARE BLUNT

After Deer won his antlers, he looked very good wearing them. He held his head up so high and looked so handsome that Rabbit, who was still sore at having his trick discovered, decided to get even. He thought a great deal about what sort of trick would be best to play on Deer, and at last he had what he thought was a pretty good idea.

One day, when he saw Deer in the woods, he stretched a large grapevine across the trail and then chewed it as Rabbit can do, until it was very nearly gnawed through in the middle. He waited until he saw Deer coming. Then he backed up a bit, took a good run at the vine, and jumped at it, snapping his teeth very loudly as he jumped. He kept running and jumping, running and jumping, until Deer, who is a very curious animal, just had to come over to find out what Rabbit was doing.

"Why, can't you see that I am practicing my jumps?" said Rabbit. "I am so strong that I can bite through this tough grapevine in a single bite!"

Deer could hardly believe that anyone could do this, much less little Rabbit. He wanted to see Rabbit do it. So Rabbit ran back, made a tremendous spring, and bit through the grapevine, right at the place where he had gnawed it thin before.

When Deer saw this, he was jealous. "Well," he said, "I guess if you can do that, then I could do it too!" So Rabbit went looking until he found an even thicker grapevine. He stretched it across the trail, but, of course, he didn't bother to gnaw on this one at all. Deer backed up as he had seen Rabbit do. He ran as hard as he could and made a big leap right at the middle of the vine. But it snapped back and threw him right on his head! Deer kept running and jumping

· ·

and being bounced until he was all bruised!

"There must be something wrong with your teeth," said Rabbit when Deer stopped to catch his breath. "If you would like, I will take a look for you to see if I can fix the problem." By now, Deer was angry. He was determined to do this thing that Rabbit had made look so easy. So he opened his mouth wide and showed Rabbit his teeth, which in those days were long like Wolf's teeth, though not nearly so sharp.

"That's the problem, all right," said Rabbit. "No wonder you can't do it. Your teeth are too blunt to bite anything as thick as this grapevine. You should let me sharpen them so that they look like mine!" And Rabbit showed Deer his teeth. "My teeth are so sharp that I can cut a stick as well as a knife can." Rabbit showed Deer a black locust twig, which Rabbit loves to gnaw. The twig was shaved just as though it had been sharpened with a knife.

By now Deer was so eager to prove that he could do anything Rabbit could do, he forgot to be suspicious. He thought it would be a fine idea to let Rabbit sharpen his teeth. So Rabbit looked all

· ·

around until he found just the sort of rock he was searching for, a hard stone with rough edges. He began filing and filing away on Deer's teeth.

"Oh, oh, that hurts!" said Deer.

"Well, yes, it always hurts a little right at first," said Rabbit. "That just means they are starting to get sharp!" So Deer kept quiet and let Rabbit work. Rabbit filed and filed until Deer's teeth were worn down right to the gums. "Now, try that," said Rabbit. Deer tried again, but his teeth were so worn down, he could hardly bite at all!

"Now you've paid for your fine antlers!" said Rabbit, and he bounded away through the bushes, laughing and laughing. Since that time, Deer's teeth are so blunt, he cannot eat anything but grass and leaves.

Rabbit Helps Wildcat Hunt Turkeys

Long ago, in the days when all creatures still spoke the same language, Rabbit was walking through the woods, listening to the birds sing. Unfortunately, he was not paying enough attention to what was around him, and Wildcat was able to spring on him and catch him.

"Ho, Rabbit!" said Wildcat. "You will now be my dinner!"

Rabbit thought very quickly and said to Wildcat, "I am too small and scrawny to be more than a mouthful for such a mighty animal as you. You deserve to eat better. Let me go, and I will show you where you can get a whole drove of turkeys!"

RABBIT HELPS WILDCAT HUNT TURKEYS

. . . .

"Turkeys are wily and hard to catch," said Wildcat. "I have already caught you."

"But I hunt turkeys often," said Rabbit. "I will show you what to do." So Wildcat let Rabbit up and followed him through the woods. Soon, looking through the trees, they could see a great many turkeys.

"Do as I say," said Rabbit. "Lie down as if you were dead and do not move, even if I kick you. When I give you the word, jump up and catch as many turkeys as you can!" Wildcat agreed and stretched out as if he were dead. Rabbit gathered rotten wood and crumbled it over Wildcat's eyes and nose so he would look as if he had been dead for some time.

Then Rabbit walked over to the turkeys, calling, "Brothers, come and see! I have found our old enemy, Wildcat. He is lying dead on the trail, and I think it would be good to have a dance over him!" At first the turkeys were very nervous about going anywhere near Wildcat even if he was dead, but at last Rabbit convinced them to come and look at poor Wildcat lying dead on the road.

Rabbit said, "You know I have a good singing voice and I am

often the dance leader, so I will show you what to do. I will lead the song, and you dance in a circle around him." Since the turkeys could see Wildcat, they believed he was really dead. He had killed so many of them in the past that they thought it was a fine idea to dance over him now that he couldn't kill them anymore.

Rabbit picked up a stick and began to beat time, singing:
"*Galagi 'na hasuyak,'*
Galagi 'na hasuyak,'
Pick out your gobbler,
Pick out your gobbler."

"Why do you sing in that way?" asked the oldest turkey.

"Oh, that's just the way that Wildcat used to do it," said Rabbit. "So that's what we should sing over him."

Rabbit started the song again, and the turkeys began to dance in a circle around Wildcat. "Closer, dance closer," said Rabbit, "and I will sing louder." When they had danced around several times, Rabbit said, "Now you must rush up to him and hit him, the way we do in the war dance!"

RABBIT HELPS WILDCAT HUNT TURKEYS

· ·

The turkeys, thinking that Wildcat was surely dead, all rushed up to him and began to kick him. Rabbit drummed as hard as he could and sang his loudest:

"Pick out your gobbler,

Pick out your gobbler!"

Wildcat jumped up and caught several fat turkeys. He let Rabbit go and had himself a fine meal. And Rabbit went on about some other mischief.

RABBIT GOES DUCK HUNTING

Now, Rabbit was so boastful that he would claim to be able to do whatever anyone else could do, and he was so tricky that he could usually make the other animals believe it all. He was especially jealous of Otter because the other animals had chosen Otter's fur coat as the most beautiful.

Once Rabbit claimed that he could swim in the water and eat fish as Otter did. The animals told him to prove it. Rabbit took them to a marshy place on the river, and they watched as he slid into the water. Rabbit stayed under as long as he could, gulping water and nibbling on river mud. When he came up, his belly was so swollen and his breath was so bad that even Otter was fooled.

Soon afterward, Rabbit and Otter met again, and Otter said, "I eat ducks sometimes."

"Oh," said Rabbit, "I often eat ducks too."

"Well," said Otter, "since you like ducks, we should catch and eat some together." Rabbit agreed, so they went up the river until they saw several large ducks in the water. They crept closer to the ducks without being seen.

"You go first," said Rabbit. Otter dove from the bank and swam underwater until he reached the ducks. He pulled one down and swam back to Rabbit, and the other ducks never even noticed.

"Now," said Rabbit, "watch and see how I hunt ducks!" Rabbit peeled bark from a sapling and braided it into a strong noose. Then he went into the river and began to swim underwater as he had seen Otter do. But he could only go a little way before he was nearly choking, and he had to come to the surface to breathe. He went under again and came up a little closer to the ducks. He took a deep breath and dove under, and this time he was able to swim up among the ducks.

Quickly, Rabbit threw his noose over the head of the largest duck and caught him. The duck began to squawk and thrash in the water, and Rabbit was shaken almost senseless. He hung on, however, and at last the duck spread his wings and flew into the sky, with Rabbit still dangling from the noose! As loud as he could, Rabbit called back to Otter, "Before I eat ducks, I often like to fly with them in this way!" Otter watched in amazement as the two sailed on out of sight.

Now, the duck Rabbit had chosen was very large and strong. He flew on and on. At last, when he showed no sign of landing, Rabbit was forced to let go of the braided rope. He fell down and down and landed in a tall, hollow sycamore stump. There was no hole in the bottom of the stump from which to escape, so Rabbit was trapped. He stayed there until he was so hungry that he began to eat his own fur, as he does to this day when he is starving.

After several days, when Rabbit was weak from hunger, he heard the sound of children playing nearby. Quickly, Rabbit began to sing to them, "Cut a door here and look at me. I'm the prettiest thing you

ever did see!" The children ran home to get their father. He came to the tree and heard Rabbit singing. He began to chop a hole in the base of the tree stump, and Rabbit sang louder, "Cut it larger so you can see me better. I'm the prettiest thing you'll ever see!"

They kept chopping until Rabbit decided the hole was big enough to allow him to escape. Rabbit called to the people, "Stand back from the hole so you can see me better. You'll want a good look when I come out!" They stood back from the hole, and Rabbit jumped out and dashed away. He did not learn his lesson, though. Rabbit is still just as boastful as ever.

Rabbit and the Tar Wolf

A long time ago, a great drought came over the land. The creeks and the rivers were dry, and there was no more water in the lakes. The animals were having a very hard time of it and at last they held a council to decide what to do. After much talk, it was announced that they must all work together to dig a well to see them through the dry spell.

Now, Rabbit is a very lazy fellow, and this sounded like hard work to him. So he stood up in the council house and began to speak. "I do not think it is right for me to dig in the dirt," said Rabbit. "My paws will get dirty, and as you can see, they are very pretty just as

they are. Besides, everyone knows that I am a small animal and don't drink much. I can get by with the dewdrops on the grass!"

The others were not very happy with Rabbit's words, and they told him that he could not share in the water if he would not share in the work. But Rabbit insisted that he could take care of himself, and he sat in the shade and watched as the other animals dug the well. At last it was done, and all the animals took turns drinking a small amount of water every day.

As the days passed and the dry weather continued, all the animals noticed that Rabbit stayed just as sleek and sassy as ever. "It is the dewdrops," said Rabbit. "I can get more than enough water in that way." But as time went on, the other animals began to see that the level of water in the public well was a little lower each day. They began to suspect that Rabbit was stealing water at night when they were all sleeping.

The other animals went to Wolf and Fox and told them the way their thoughts were going. Wolf and Fox offered to find a way to catch Rabbit in the act of stealing water. So Wolf and Fox gathered spruce gum and pine tar from the trees. They shaped and molded it until they had made a large tar wolf. Then they set it up near the well so that it looked as if the tar wolf was standing guard over the water.

Late that night, Rabbit came to the well to drink enough water to last him through the next day, for as the animals suspected, Rabbit had been coming to the well every night. When he saw the queer black animal there, at first he was frightened and did not move. "Who's there?" he called. The tar wolf, of course, made no answer, and Rabbit grew bolder. "You must tell me who you are," Rabbit called again. When the tar wolf made no sound and did not move, Rabbit grew braver still. He came closer and said, "You get out of my way or I will hit you!" Still the tar wolf did not move, so Rabbit drew back his paw and hit the tar wolf as hard as he could. His paw caught in the sticky gum, and Rabbit was stuck.

Now he was really angry, and he said, "Let me go or I will kick you!" Then Rabbit struck again with his hind foot, so hard that he was caught fast and could not even move. There he stayed until

Grandmother Sun rose the next morning and all the other animals came to the well.

When the animals found Rabbit stuck to the tar wolf, they teased him and laughed at him, and had great fun making sport of him for a while. Then they decided to kill him for a thief.

Everyone had an idea about how to kill Rabbit, but finally it was decided that they should cut off his head. When Rabbit heard this, he began to laugh. "Go ahead," said Rabbit, still laughing. "Didn't you know that when I go to sleep at night, I take off my head and put it on a shelf? I have often had my head off, and it does not hurt me."

This made the other animals unhappy, until someone else suggested that Rabbit should be burned in the fire. Rabbit laughed and laughed. "Go ahead," said Rabbit. "Fire does not hurt me. I often go into the fire for myself. Fire feels good to me!"

They went on in this way for some time. Every way that was proposed to kill Rabbit made him laugh harder and insist that it was useless. At last, Fox said that maybe it would be good to throw him so deep into the briar thicket that he would never find his way out.

. . . .

At that, Rabbit began to cry and beg and plead with them, saying that he would get lost and starve. The others were delighted to see Rabbit finally afraid of something, so they hurried to do as Fox had suggested.

They threw Rabbit as far and as hard as they could. But when Rabbit landed in the briar thicket, he whooped and bounded away, calling back to his enemies, "Didn't you know? This briar thicket is where I live!" And so once again, Rabbit was free to create some other mischief.

RABBIT RACES WITH TURTLE

It is true that Rabbit loved to brag and exaggerate about all the things he could do, but one thing that everyone agreed on was that he was a very fast runner. Turtle loved to boast too, however, and one day he told the people that he was even faster than Rabbit. Rabbit heard about Turtle's claim, and they began to argue so fiercely that everyone agreed the only way to settle the matter was to have a race between the two. It was decided that Turtle and Rabbit would race over four mountain ridges, and the one who came over the fourth ridge first would be the winner.

Now, no one had ever seen Turtle move at anything but the slowest of paces, so Rabbit was certain of his ability to win. So sure was he

· ·

that he told Turtle, "You know you can't run. You could never win a race with me. I will give you the first ridge. You will have to cross only three, while I cross all four."

Turtle agreed to Rabbit's terms, but that night he called together all his turtle relatives. "You must help me put an end to Rabbit's boasting," said Turtle. He explained his plan to his family, and they all agreed to help.

When the day of the race came, all the animals gathered. Some came to the starting point to see the runners off. Others waited on the fourth ridge to declare the winner. Rabbit came to the starting point, but Turtle had gone ahead to the next ridge as Rabbit had arranged. The others could just see his shiny back through the long grass. The signal was given, and the race began! Rabbit burst from the starting point with his long jumps, expecting to win the race before Turtle could even make it down his first ridge. Imagine his surprise when he came to the top of the ridge and saw Turtle disappearing over the top of the next mountain!

Rabbit ran even faster, and when he came to the top of the sec-

. . . .

ond mountain, he looked all around, expecting to see Turtle somewhere in the long grass. He looked up—and there was the sun glinting off Turtle's shell as he crossed the third ridge! Now Rabbit was truly surprised, and he was beginning to be worried. He gave his longest jumps ever to catch up. When he reached the top of the third ridge, he was so tired and out of breath he could only fall over and cry as he watched Turtle cross the fourth mountain and win the race!

The other animals gave the race to Turtle, and everyone wondered how slow Turtle had managed to beat Rabbit. Turtle just smiled and never spoke of it, but it was really very easy. All Turtle's relatives look just alike, so Turtle had placed one near the top of each ridge. Whenever Rabbit had come into sight, a Turtle relative had crawled to the top of the mountain ahead of him and then hidden in the tall grass. Turtle, himself, had climbed the fourth ridge to cross the finish line.

So Turtle won the race with a very good trick of his own. But if he had hoped to stop Rabbit's bragging, he was surely disappointed. No one has ever been able to do that.

Bear Dines with Rabbit

In the days when the different kinds of animals could still talk to one another, Bear invited Rabbit to dinner. He had been to a dance and heard Rabbit sing, and he had enjoyed it so much that he wanted to do something nice for Rabbit. And so he had said, "Tomorrow, come to my house. We will eat together."

Now, everyone knew how much Bear likes to eat, and Rabbit thought, "He will surely have lots of good food. I should go." So the next day, Rabbit went to Bear's house. Bear had a great pot of beans cooking on the fire. They visited for a while as the beans cooked, and Rabbit was enjoying himself very much. Finally Bear tasted the beans to see if they were done.

"These beans taste a little dry to me," said Bear. "But don't worry, I can fix that. Some grease will make them taste better." Rabbit watched in amazement as Bear took a sharp knife, cut his side, and let the oil run into the pot! When the beans were finished cooking, Rabbit and Bear ate. Sure enough, the beans were delicious!

When Rabbit saw Bear do this thing, he was jealous. It was Rabbit's nature to think, "I can do that too!" whenever he saw someone else's magic. So when they had finished eating, Rabbit said, "I must repay your kindness, Bear. Tomorrow, you come to my house and I will cook for you."

The next day, Bear went to visit Rabbit. Proudly, Rabbit said, "I am cooking beans too. Now I'll get the grease for them." So saying, Rabbit took a knife and drove it into his side! But instead of oil, out gushed a stream of blood. Rabbit fell over, fainting, and nearly died.

Bear is a good doctor, but it was hard work to tie up the wound in Rabbit's side and stop the bleeding. When Rabbit was feeling better, Bear scolded him, saying, "You can't do everything you see

someone else do, Rabbit! Can't you see that I am large and strong and lined with thick fat all over? That little knife can't hurt me! You are little and lean. From now on, you stick to the tricks you know!"

Bear gave Rabbit very good advice, but of course Rabbit never listened. He went on about some other mischief.

Rabbit Steals from Fox

Once, as Rabbit was making his way through the woods, he met Fox coming down the trail carrying a great load of fish. Rabbit had often boasted of his ability to catch and eat fish. But the truth was that Rabbit had never even tasted fish! So Rabbit was very friendly to Fox. He was hoping Fox would share some fish with him.

After they had walked together for a ways, Rabbit said, "Since you have so many fish there, I would be glad to help you eat them."

But Fox said, "Rabbit, I must carry these fish home to my family. My wife and children will be hungry."

. . . .

"Oh, that's all right," said Rabbit. "I ate fish just the other day, anyway."

Now, that's what Rabbit *said*, but what he was thinking was: "I'll find a way to get some fish." Rabbit thought about it, and soon he had what he thought was a good idea. He walked on a ways with Fox, and then he said, "Well, since you don't need my help carrying your fish, I'll leave you on this trail. My home is over that way."

Rabbit left the trail and, in the way Rabbit has, scurried through the thick brush so that he came out on the trail ahead of Fox. Rabbit rolled in the dust so that his fur was matted and dirty; then he lay down next to the trail and pretended to be dead. Pretty soon, Fox walked by, carrying his fish. "Oh, look," said Fox. "Here is a dead rabbit." But Fox was carrying such a heavy load of fish that he had no interest in one dead rabbit, and he walked on by.

As soon as Fox had passed, Rabbit jumped up and scurried through the brush. When he was ahead of Fox once more, he lay down by the trail again. Here came Fox, still carrying his fish. "Well," said Fox, "another dead rabbit! If I did not have so many

HOW RABBIT TRICKED OTTER

fish, I would carry these rabbits home to my family." And again, he passed by.

Rabbit scurried through the brush, and again he came out on the trail just ahead of Fox. This time, he stretched out across the trail so Fox would have to stop. Sure enough, when Fox saw the third "dead" rabbit, he came to a stop and set his fish down. "Well," said Fox, "three rabbits will make a nice stew. With three rabbits and all these fish, my family will not be hungry for many days." So Fox hid his fish by the side of the trail, then hurried back to pick up the other two rabbits.

When Fox came back to the place where he had seen the second rabbit, there was nothing there! "Oh, well," thought Fox, "someone else must have taken it. I can still make a stew with two rabbits." And he hurried further down the trail to the place where he had seen the first "dead" rabbit. But when he reached that spot, there was nothing there, either! "Someone has certainly been greedy, carrying off both rabbits that way!" thought Fox. "At least I still have one rabbit and all my fish!"

· · · · · · · · · · · · · · · ·

But, of course, when Fox retraced his steps, he found the third "dead" rabbit had vanished, along with all the fish! There was nothing for Fox to do but make his way home empty-handed, knowing his wife would be angry. And so she was.

Meanwhile, Rabbit took all the fish that Fox had caught. He carried them a long way away from the trail where he had left Fox. Then he sat down and cooked and ate every one of those fish! "Well," said Rabbit when he was full, "I don't think fish are so very tasty after all. I wonder why people go to so much trouble to catch them!" And Rabbit never bothered to "go fishing" again.

RABBIT SENDS WOLF TO THE SUNSET

One time, long ago, Rabbit and Wolf went hunting together. Just as the sun was starting to set, they managed to catch a small cow. It was a very small cow, but Wolf and Rabbit were both pleased because they were so hungry. In fact, Rabbit was *so* hungry, he began at once to think of a way to keep all the meat for himself! "After all," Rabbit thought, "Wolf was not very much help. I could have caught that cow for myself if he had just gone about his own business!"

As the sun was sinking, there was a great red blaze in the west, and this gave Rabbit an idea. "Ho, Wolf," said Rabbit. "Since we shared in the hunt, we should share in the work of preparing the meal. I will do the hard work this time. I will cut up the meat and get it ready for cooking. Why don't you run over and borrow some fire from those people in the west?" And he pointed to the red glow of the sunset.

Wolf was very pleased and surprised to hear Rabbit offer to work so hard, so he set off at once to borrow the fire. He went down the hill and then climbed to the top of the next ridge. When he got to the top, he could see that he still had some distance to go to reach the red area he thought was fire. Again, he went downhill and then up-hill, but the fire was still very far away! Wolf continued to travel, up one hill and down the next, but the fire was still no closer. Wolf could see that the red glow was growing dimmer. "Oh no," thought Wolf, "the fire is going out." He ran as fast as he could, until he was so tired he could barely stand. Finally, as Wolf watched from the top of a hill, the red glow disappeared completely.

Sadly, Wolf turned and began to walk back the way he had come. "Oh, well," thought Wolf, "Rabbit and I will just have to build our own fire."

RABBIT SENDS WOLF TO THE SUNSET

Now as soon as Wolf had gone to get fire, Rabbit got very busy. He cut up the meat and hid it very carefully. Then he cut off the cow's tail and buried it in the ground so that just the hairy tip was sticking out of the dirt. As soon as he saw Wolf returning, Rabbit took hold of the tail and pretended to pull with all his might. "Quick, Brother Wolf," yelled Rabbit. "This cow is getting away! She has gone under the ground! Help me pull her out!"

Wolf rushed to help Rabbit. He grabbed hold of the tail with Rabbit and gave a mighty jerk, and the tail popped out of the earth! But, of course, there was nothing on the end of the tail. Pretending to be greatly disappointed, Rabbit gave the tail to Wolf. "Since I am the one who let the cow go underground," said Rabbit, "you should at least have this tail to eat."

And Rabbit went off to find his meat, while Wolf was left with a very poor supper!

RABBIT DANCES WITH THE PEOPLE

A long time ago, there was a young man who was ashamed of his face. He had quite a nice face, but for some reason he felt he was ugly. He was a very good artist, though, and he hit on the idea of carving a mask for himself. This mask was very handsome, and the boy felt very good when he had it on. He wore the mask to all the dances, and the people thought it was his natural face.

Now, there were seven young women who were enchanted with the face on the mask. They watched for the young man at all the dances. They would talk to the boy between rounds of songs, and each thought of him as a special friend.

One night Rabbit was hiding in the bushes and watching the people dance. He had come hoping to learn some new songs. He watched the young man with all the pretty girls following him, and, as usual, Rabbit was jealous. He thought, "I would like to be that young fellow!"

After the dance, Rabbit followed the young man to his house, hoping to learn some of his attracting medicine. Imagine his surprise when he saw the boy take off his face! "Ho," thought Rabbit, "that mask must be his secret!" Right away, Rabbit began scheming to get his hands on the boy's mask. He watched very carefully to see where the boy hid it.

Some time later, Rabbit heard about a big dance the people were planning, and he made up his mind to go. In the middle of the night, when everything was dark, Rabbit crept into the young man's house and stole away with the mask.

The next night, Rabbit dressed in his finest dance clothes, put on the mask, and headed out to where the people were dancing. At first he was having a fine time. Rabbit was a good dancer, and the seven young women gave him a warm welcome. But after a time the girls said, "We're tired of dancing. Come sit and talk with us." So Rabbit followed the young women to a place where they could sit and talk.

"It is a fine night for a dance," Rabbit began, but he broke off when he saw the girls staring at him in amazement.

"My friend," said one young woman, "what has happened to your voice? It is so high and squeaky!"

"Oh," said Rabbit, thinking quickly, "I choked on a bone caught in my throat yesterday. Perhaps that is what makes my voice so scratchy!"

But the girls were suspicious. "And why have you stayed away from us for so long?" asked another.

"Well," said Rabbit, "that is just because I have been away on some very important business!"

"Then who was that dancing with us just last night?" cried the girls. They began to giggle and pinch Rabbit until he was black and blue all over! Suddenly, the mask slipped sideways and the girls saw

. . . .

Rabbit's face. "Oh, this is just Rabbit, up to his tricks!" cried the girls. And they chased him away from the dance ground.

When Rabbit was safely away from the angry young women, he threw the mask down and headed home. "I do not think I will ever dance with those people again," thought Rabbit. "They have a lot to learn about good manners!"

Meanwhile, the young man was very worried when he discovered that his mask was missing. He searched and searched until he found it on the ground where Rabbit had dropped it. Happily, he put the mask on and hurried to the dance ground. He was very surprised when he saw the way the young women treated him, though. They would not even talk to him! Whenever he came near, they called him names and ran away!

At last, the young man thought to put away the mask and go to the dance wearing his own face. To his surprise, he discovered the young women liked him very much, just the way he was.

WHAT BECAME OF RABBIT

Now, Deer never forgave Rabbit for filing his teeth down, and he was always very angry with him. But he never let Rabbit know about his anger. He was always very friendly to him. Deer was waiting for just the right time to take his revenge.

One day, as Deer and Rabbit were walking along and talking, they came to a small stream. Rabbit was a great jumper, so Deer said, "Let's race and see who can jump over that stream! When I say *Ku!* we will both run and jump."

Rabbit loved to race, so he eagerly accepted Deer's proposal.

WHAT BECAME OF RABBIT

· ·

When Deer said *Ku!* Rabbit ran and jumped as high as he could. But Deer stopped on the bank of the stream, and when Rabbit landed on the other side, Deer conjured the stream into a great ocean! Rabbit was stuck on the other side, and all the rabbits we know now are merely Rabbit's descendants.

Of course, this all happened a long time ago, and Rabbit knew a great many tricks of his own. It could be that Rabbit found his way back into this world. He may be singing and dancing or playing a trick on someone right this very moment.

GAYLE ROSS is a direct descendant of John Ross, the principal chief of the Cherokee nation during the infamous "Trail of Tears." For over a decade, she has told the myths and legends of the Cherokee people at schools, colleges, and festivals across the United States and Canada, carrying on a family tradition begun by her grandmother. She has long wanted to gather the tribal stories about Rabbit, the central figure in Cherokee folklore. Gayle notes that all stories change as they travel through time and tellers. She offers these to honor the ancestors and to reach the children. Gayle lives in Fredericksburg, Texas.

MURV JACOB is a painter-pipemaker of Kentucky-Cherokee descent. He has won numerous awards for his work, including the Grand Award at the Trail of Tears Art Show. He lives with his wife and children in Tahlequah, Oklahoma.